River Rose

and the Magical Lullaby

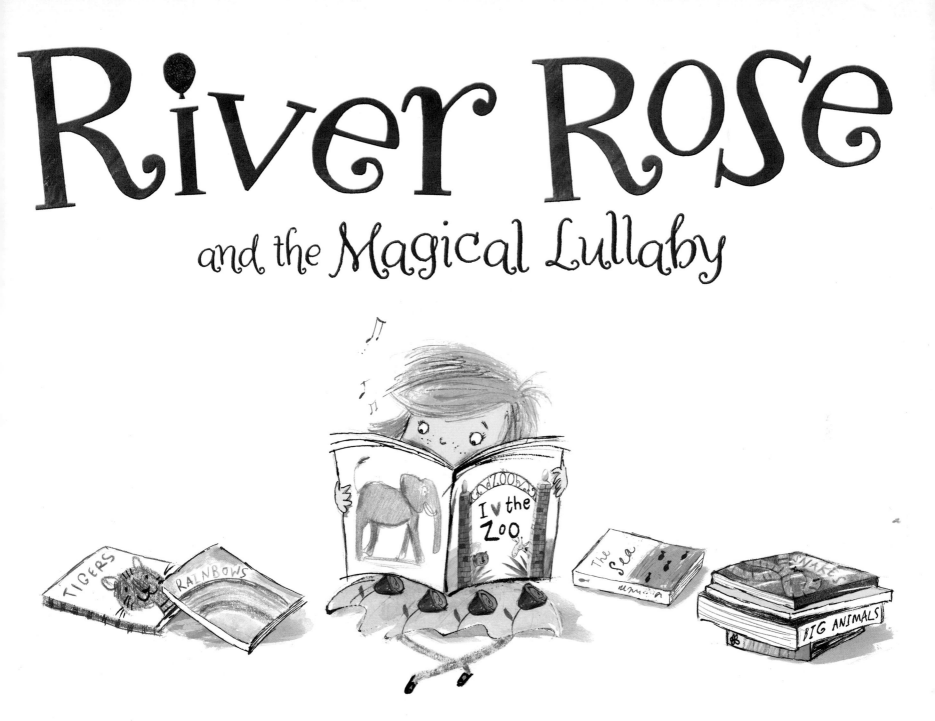

Kelly Clarkson

illustrated by Laura Hughes

HARPER

An Imprint of HarperCollinsPublishers

ISBN 978-0-06-242756-4

The artist used ink, paint, and collage to create the illustrations for this book.
Typography by Whitney Manger
16 17 18 19 20   SCP   10 9 8 7 6 5 4 3 2 1
❖
First Edition

This book is dedicated to my mother, Jeanne. She taught me the value of education and the thrill of escaping into an adventure by introducing me to the mysteries of the Boxcar Children and the magic of *Matilda*. She embraced the dreamer in me. May we all be dreamers and never stop believing in magic—just like River Rose.

—K.C.

River Rose loves to sing. She loves to make new friends.
She skips and hops, she beeps and bops, she loves to play pretend.

Her best friend's name is Joplin. He loves to be-bop too.

And tomorrow for the first time, they're going to the zoo!

"Oh, Joplin! I'm so excited. I cannot wait to see
lions that roar and seals that bark—
how long can one night be?"

River Rose tossed and turned. She wouldn't close her eyes
until her mom came in and sang to her this lullaby:

Every night you lie with me.
When I wake you're still here.
I don't know if I ever could find
someone as kind and dear.
No one gets me like you do;
you can tell by my smile.
I'm gonna miss you so much while you sleep.
But know that I'm by your side.

A squeaky sound woke River Rose in the middle of the night.

Outside her bedroom window something gave her quite a fright.

She sat up straight and there she saw in front of the shiny moon
a bobbling, wobbling handful of magical balloons!

Soon she was flying and swooshing through the sky
on the adventure of a lifetime, with Joplin by her side.

Then she landed down in the center of the zoo.
And right around the corner came a bouncy kangaroo.

He was just about to ask if there was something he could do
when River Rose jumped up and said, "We've come to play with you!"

She turned on all the lights and sang, "There's so much I want to see. Lions, tiger, bears, oh my! . . . Let's have a zoo party!"

The elephants got things started,
spraying water in the air.
River Rose danced around
and got soaked without a care.

Next she joined the penguins, slip-sliding in the snow.
The zebras and giraffes joined in and put on quite a show!

Then she asked the turtles, "Can I join you in the water?"

She hopped from pad to pad and played tag with an otter.

Oh no! A rock below began to shimmy and to shake.

"Wait! That's not a rock at all!

There's a hippo in the lake!"

She saw an ice-cream shop ahead and asked was it okay
to go and build herself a *GI*-normous fudge sundae.

River Rose and Joplin continued through the zoo.

She turned and asked her best friend, "What do YOU want to do?"

Joplin took off running right for the merry-go-round.
They rode the ride a hundred times, falling dizzy to the ground.

The polar bears were waiting, playing quietly in the snow.
She asked if she could join them, but they had to let her know,
"We're really all so tired now—polar bears need their sleep.
The trick to fun is to let the day be done.
That's the secret that we keep."

River Rose realized then it was time to say good-bye.
And as the bears snuggled in their den,
she remembered the lullaby:

Every night you lie with me.
When I wake you're still here.
I don't know if I ever could find
someone as kind and dear.

Through the window and then back to bed,
a big smile upon her face.
"That was a great adventure—
but home is my favorite place!"